D0633432

Spooked

TRACKING GHOSTS

BY EMILY RAIJ

Reading Consultant:

Barbara J. Fox
Professor Emerita
North Carolina State University

CAPSTONE PRESS
a capstone imprint

Blazers Books are published by Capstone Press,
1710 Roe Crest Drive, North Mankato, Minnesota 56003
www.capstonepub.com

Library of Congress Cataloging-in-Publication Data
Raij, Emily, author.
 Tracking ghosts / by Emily Raij.
    pages cm. — (Blazers books. Spooked!)
 Summary: "Describes tools and methods used by ghost hunters, including examples of ghost
hunters' paranormal experiences"— Provided by publisher.
 Audience: Ages 8-14
 Audience: Grades 4 to 6
 ISBN 978-1-4914-4078-0 (library binding)
 ISBN 978-1-4914-4112-1 (ebook pdf)
1. Ghosts—Juvenile literature. 2. Parapsychology—Investigation—Juvenile literature. I. Title.
 BF1461.R344 2016
 133.1—dc23
                                        2015001334

Editorial Credits
Anna Butzer, editor; Kyle Grenz, designer; Morgan Walters, media researcher; Kathy McColley,
production specialist

Photo Credits
Alamy: William Attard McCarthy, 10, 11; Dreamstime: Guarant, 18, 19, Photographerlondon, 22, 23,
Welcomia, (Magic park) background 2, 3, 30, 31, 32, Carla F. Castagno, 15; Getty Images: belterz,
16, 17; iStockphoto: inhauscreative, (ghost hunters) cover, inhauscreative, 9, JohnGollop, (blurred
ghost) 12, 13, piranka, 1; Newscom: oseph Kaczmarek/ZUMAPRESS, 6, 7, SUN/Newscom, 26, 27;
Shutterstock: D_D, (vintage photo frames and paper) throughout, (paper notes) throughout, Everett
Historical, (little girl ghosts) bottom right 13, Lario Tus, (womens ghost) cover, Mariusz Niedzwiedzki,
24, 25, Radek Sturgolewski, 28, 29, Sarah2, 5, Sean Nel, 20, 21, Sociologas, (photo strip) throughout,
Tueris, (black vector stains) throughout

Printed in China by Nordica
0415/CA21500562
032015   008844NORDF15

TABLE OF CONTENTS

COULD IT BE A GHOST?

You see strange sights, hear creaking stairs, and feel a chill in the air. Is it just your imagination, or could it be a ghost? Some people believe ghosts haunt different places. Decide for yourself!

A GHOST HUNTER'S JOB

Ghost hunters collect **evidence** about mysterious events. These **paranormal investigators** ask questions about strange sights and sounds. They use many tools to study hauntings.

evidence—information, items, and facts that help prove something to be true or false

paranormal investigator—someone who studies events that science can't explain

DID YOU KNOW?

Ghost hunters must ask home owners and building owners for permission to investigate.

TRACKING TOOLS

A camera, notebook, and pen are good tools to begin an investigation. Most ghost hunters also bring a flashlight, sound recorder, and video camera. Some ghost hunters use **thermometers** to measure changes in room temperature.

thermometer—a tool that measures temperature

WHAT CAMERAS CAPTURE

Photos sometimes show dark shadows or glowing lights. These things may not have been seen when the photos were taken. Glowing **orbs** may also appear in pictures.

DID YOU KNOW?

Some investigators believe glowing orbs in photos could be **spirits**.

orb—a glowing ball of light that sometimes appears in photographs taken at reportedly haunted locations

spirit—the soul or invisible part of a person that is believed to control thoughts and feelings

FAKE PHOTOS

Skeptics think photos of ghosts are fake. Some skeptics say that people use computers to put objects in pictures. Dust or small bugs on the **lens** of a camera can cause strange images. A camera's flash can also create odd lights or double images.

skeptic—a person who questions things that other people believe to be true

lens—a piece of curved glass in a camera that bends light and focuses images

DID YOU KNOW?

You can see through some double images in photos. This camera trick makes the images look ghostly!

TEMPERATURE TESTS

Some people feel chilly in haunted places. Ghost hunters say spirits can make a room feel cooler. Paranormal investigators believe ghosts use the heat energy around them to become visible. Could a cold room mean a ghost is nearby?

DID YOU KNOW?

Some ghost hunters use **thermal** cameras to record temperature changes in a room. Some thermal cameras add color to images to help show different temperatures.

thermal—having to do with heat or holding in heat

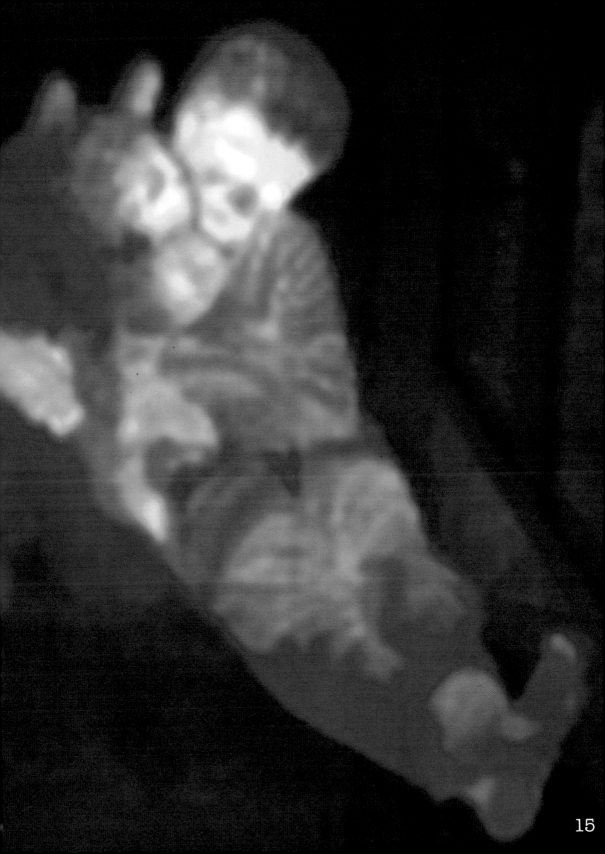

ENVIRONMENTAL EXPLANATIONS

There are many simple causes for cool spots in a room. Old houses may be poorly heated. Doors and windows can have cracks that let in cooler air. Sometimes temperatures drop suddenly or only in certain spots. Ghost hunters say this is harder to explain and could mean ghosts!

SPOOKY SOUNDS

Ghost hunters have recorded noises that sound like human voices. Humans cannot make some of the sounds ghost hunters have recorded. Ghost hunters say these noises could prove ghosts exist.

DID YOU KNOW?

Ghostly voices in the background of recordings are called electronic voice **phenomena** or EVPs.

phenomena—very unusual or remarkable events

HEARING THE TRUTH

Skeptics say ghostly sounds may come from pipes, mice, or bugs in the walls. Animals, tree branches, and wind make creepy noises. Radio and TV **signals** can also cause strange sounds.

signal—a radio, sound, or light wave that sends information from one place to another

21

ASKING QUESTIONS

Some people make up ghost stories for attention. Ghost hunters must decide who is telling the truth. Ghost hunters interview people who have lived at a haunted location. **Research** about the history of a place also can provide helpful information.

research—to study and learn about a subject

DID YOU KNOW?

Ghost hunters suggest doing historical research after collecting evidence. This way historical information does not affect their conclusions.

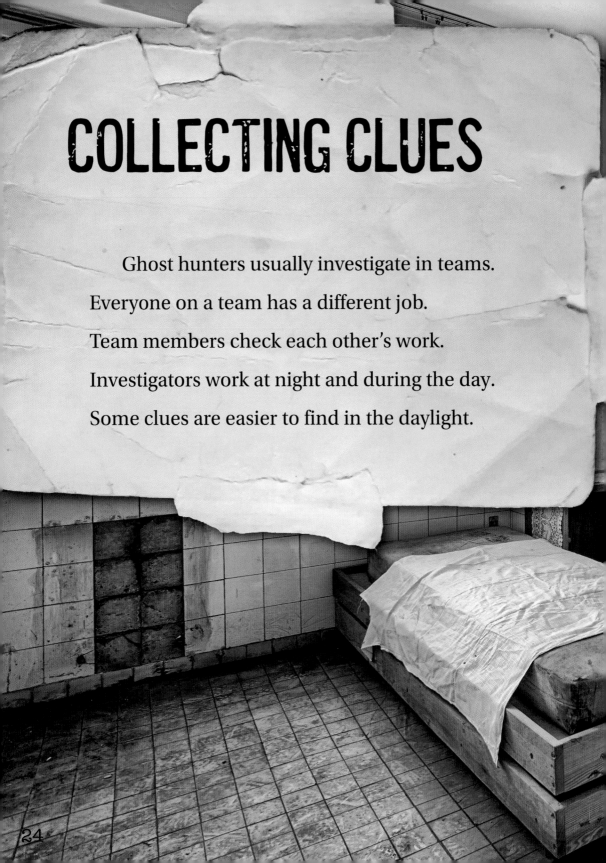

COLLECTING CLUES

Ghost hunters usually investigate in teams.

Everyone on a team has a different job.

Team members check each other's work.

Investigators work at night and during the day.

Some clues are easier to find in the daylight.

DID YOU KNOW?

Sometimes ghost hunters investigate an area in the daylight first. They look for anything dangerous that might not be visible at night.

EXAMINING THE EVIDENCE

It can take hours to look at videos and listen to sound recordings. Many times there is not good **proof** of hauntings. Ghost hunters always try to find natural causes for hauntings. The ghost-hunting team must talk about the clues and decide.

DID YOU KNOW?

There are many books, TV shows, and movies about ghost hunting. You can even take tours of places said to be haunted!

proof—facts or evidence that something is true or false

NATURAL CAUSES

Most of the time, strange images and sounds have natural causes. Animals, weather, and camera tricks can make ghost stories seem real! Even after collecting clues we may not have an explanation. But we can still have fun going on a ghost hunt!

GLOSSARY

evidence (EV-uh-duhnss)—information, items, and facts that help prove something to be true or false

lens (LENZ)—a piece of curved glass in a camera that bends light and focuses images

orb (ORB)—a glowing ball of light that sometimes appears in photographs taken at reportedly haunted locations

paranormal investigator (pa-ruh-NOR-muhl in-VESS-tuh-gate-ur)—someone who studies events that science can't explain

phenomena (fe-NOM-uh-nuh)—very unusual or remarkable events

proof (PROOF)—facts or evidence that something is true or false

research (REE-surch)—to study and learn about a subject

signal (SIG-nuhl)—a radio, sound, or light wave that sends information from one place to another

skeptic (SKEP-tik)—a person who questions things that other people believe to be true

spirit (SPIHR-it)—the soul or invisible part of a person that is believed to control thoughts and feelings

thermal (THUR-muhl)—having to do with heat or holding in heat

thermometer (thur-MOM-uh-tur)—a tool that measures temperature

READ MORE

Doak, Robin S. *Investigating Hauntings, Ghosts, and Poltergeists.* Unexplained Phenomena. Mankato, Minn.: Capstone Press, 2011.

Hawes, Jason, Grant Wilson, and Cameron Dokey. *Ghost Hunt: Chilling Tales of the Unknown.* New York: Little, Brown, & Co., 2010.

Martin, Michael. *The Unsolved Mystery of Ghosts.* Unexplained Mysteries. North Mankato, Minn.: Capstone Press, 2013.

INTERNET SITES

FactHound offers a safe, fun way to find Internet sites related to this book. All of the sites on FactHound have been researched by our staff.

Here's all you do:

Visit *www.facthound.com*

Type in this code: 9781491440780

Check out projects, games and lots more at
www.capstonekids.com

INDEX